Missing Pieces

Leslie Bulion

Illustrated by Janet Wilson

STECK-VAUGHN
ELEMENTARY · SECONDARY · ADULT · LIBRARY

A Harcourt Company

www.steck-vaughn.com

ISBN 0-7398-5067-9

Printed in the United States of America.

1 2 3 4 5 6 7 8 9 LB 06 05 04 03 02

Contents

Chapter 1

Missing !

Most mornings I wake up when my dog, Captain, sticks her cold, wet nose in my face. Today I woke up because Captain didn't stick her cold, wet nose in my face. It's funny how you can notice something when it's missing.

My clock said seven o'clock, and that was too early for a Saturday. I should have known then that something was wrong.

I put my pillow over my head and tried to go back to sleep. That's what I do when I don't have to go to school. Today something was keeping me awake. Something else was missing. There was no noise. The house was too quiet.

"Captain?" I called.

She didn't run into my room, but I wasn't worried. She might have gone to beg my mom for a walk. It's hard for Captain to wait for me to get up on Saturdays and Sundays. She loves her walks.

I didn't hear my mom moving around in her room. I reminded myself that it was Mom and Lou's room now. I didn't hear anyone downstairs in the kitchen, either.

The strangest thing was that I didn't hear one sound from the other side of my room. Usually, I hear nonstop noise. Today there was no talking, no singing, and no thumping. It was hard to believe. Even in his sleep, Tyrone mumbled. I rolled over and looked across the room at his bed. Tyrone wasn't in it. My new five-year-old stepbrother was off to an early start.

"Good," I said to myself. I turned over to go back to sleep.

Only it was no good trying to go back to sleep. All that quiet was keeping me awake. Being awake made me hungry. Finally, I had to give up on sleeping late. I went downstairs to take care of my growling stomach. I found a note on the kitchen table. It read:

6:55 A.M.

Dear James,
Lou and I took Captain for a run in the park. We will grab breakfast out. Please keep an eye on Tyrone when he gets up.

Love, Mom

I wondered why she wrote "when he gets up." He was already up, but where was he?

There was no way around it. The kid was a pain when he was there, and a pain when he wasn't.

I thought maybe he was hiding.

"Tyrone?" I called. "Stop playing around. It's too early for games."

Sound travels in an old house like ours, so Tyrone should have heard me. He was always making a lot of noise. I should have been able to hear him, even if he was hiding.

I stuck my head out the front door. "Tyrone?"

He wasn't in the front yard. He wasn't in the back yard, either.

My stomach growled again, louder this time. I needed to eat something.

4

"Games are only fun if both people want to play, Tyrone," I yelled.

There was still no sound.

I searched every hiding place I could think of downstairs. Then, I went up to my mom's room. Tyrone wasn't anywhere. By the time I got to my room, I was starting to get a bad feeling.

Tyrone's side of the room was too neat. The blanket was pulled up over the bed.

There weren't any crayons or books on the floor. Nothing was on his table. There was no comb, no flashlight, and no money jar. There weren't any of those toy people he always played with.

I knew what I'd find before I started opening drawers. His clothes were gone. His suitcase wasn't in the closet. I'm not sure why I looked under my bed. I didn't find Tyrone. Instead I found the two missing pieces of my favorite model ship. They were the pieces I'd thought Tyrone had taken. I sat on my bed and put my head in my hands.

This would never have happened if my mom hadn't married Tyrone's dad, Lou. Tyrone and his dad would still be living in the next state. Tyrone would be making all that noise in his own room instead of mine. He wouldn't be my new stepbrother.

He wouldn't have run away.

Chapter 2

The Trouble Starts

This all started last Sunday. That was the
day Tyrone and Lou moved in. It was the
day everything started going wrong. Captain
didn't wake me up last Sunday, either. My
mom shook me awake. She was humming.
It was too early for anyone to sound happy.

"James, get up!" my mom said.

Then Captain wiggled in front of my
mom and stuck her cold, wet nose in my face.

"Too slow," I told Captain. "I'm already
awake."

"James," Mom said again, "hurry! You haven't made space for Tyrone. Lou will be here soon with the moving truck. Push your desk across to your side and slide your dresser over. We've got to fit another bed in here!"

I wished my mom could be happy without making me share my room with a five year old. We had been just fine by ourselves since my father died. Now that I was 14, I didn't need a stepbrother. I didn't need a stepfather, either.

Mom was looking at the shelves above my desk. That look meant trouble.

"Come on, Mom," I said.

"We've already talked about this, James," she said. "Those ships have got to go. Tyrone needs some space, too."

"I have 43 model ships," I moaned. "What should I do? Hang them from the ceiling?"

My mom smiled her extra evil smile. Captain followed her downstairs.

I was still hanging ships when Mom and
Lou banged the spare bed through my
doorway. Captain and Tyrone ran in with
them. Model ships were spread all over my bed.

"Wow!" Tyrone said. He made a move
toward the ships.

I stepped in front of him. "They're easy to
break," I said.

"Hey, Tyrone," Lou said. "Let's set you up in your new room."

I felt like pointing out that it wasn't his room. It was mine. I didn't say anything, though. I just kept hanging my ships. Lou handed Tyrone some sheets and went downstairs.

While I worked, Tyrone tried to make his bed. He talked to himself the whole time.

"Here's a sheet. Okay, sheet. That's good. Now another sheet."

I rolled my eyes.

When Tyrone tried to shake out his blanket, he pulled everything onto the floor.

"This bed doesn't make up like mine," he told me.

Lou brought Tyrone's suitcase up to my room. He helped fix the blanket. "I'm going down to get your dresser," he told Tyrone.

"Can I help?" Tyrone asked.

"I think I need James for this one."

The last thing I wanted to do was leave that kid alone with my ships. But I followed Lou downstairs anyway. ⚡

When we got back, Tyrone was playing on his bed with Captain. He was making some little toy people talk to her. He was using a funny, high voice.

"Down, girl," I said.

Captain gave me a look, then she took her time getting off the bed. My own dog, what a traitor. How long had the kid been here, half an hour? Already he was teaching my dog bad habits. The ships on my bed looked okay, anyway.

When the dresser was in place, Lou helped Tyrone put away his clothes. I felt like I couldn't move in my own room. ⚡

"Let's go get some lunch," Lou said.

Tyrone jumped off his bed. The covers slid onto the floor again. "You coming?" he asked me.

"I'm not hungry," I lied. I wanted to be alone.

Tyrone puffed air into his cheeks and looked at the floor. Then he turned and went downstairs.

It took a long time to finish hanging up my ships. They looked good. And they were too high for Tyrone to reach.

There was still one ship on my bed. It was the first ship I had put together. I'd made it when I was Tyrone's age, the year my father died. It was just a bunch of colored pieces that snapped together, but it was my favorite. I knew every piece by heart. So I knew right away that two pieces were missing.

Chapter 3

A Broken Ship

"I know this will take some getting used to, James," my mom said that night while we washed dishes. "It'll get better, you'll see."

I nodded, but I thought things would only get worse.

I went into the living room. Tyrone was sitting on the floor, marching his toy people up and down Captain's back. My model ship books were lined up in a row in front of Captain. Tyrone was pretending they were houses on an invisible street.

"Let's go! Up the mountain, everybody!" Tyrone shouted.

A handful of toy people landed on
Captain's head. She didn't seem to mind.

Lou was sitting in my spot on the sofa.
A basketball game was on TV, but not the
one I wanted to watch. My mom came in
from the kitchen.

Lou asked me, "Do you like basketball,
James?"

"I've got homework,"
I said.

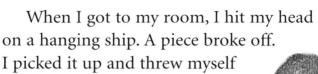

My mom raised her
eyebrows at me. On my
way upstairs, I took my
ship books away from
Tyrone's town.

When I got to my room, I hit my head
on a hanging ship. A piece broke off.
I picked it up and threw myself
on my bed.

"Do you know how
to read?"

I hadn't even been
in my room two minutes,
and already Tyrone was
up there bugging me.

I still had the broken part
of the ship in my hand. I looked
over at my desk. The ship with the
missing pieces sat there. I didn't
answer Tyrone.

"I don't know how to read," Tyrone told me.

"Then just pick up a book and pretend." I opened a book and held it in front of my face.

Tyrone was quiet, but only for about ten seconds. "I can't write yet, either," he said.

I didn't say anything.

After another minute, he spoke up again. "Can you write Greenfield?" he asked.

I put my book down.

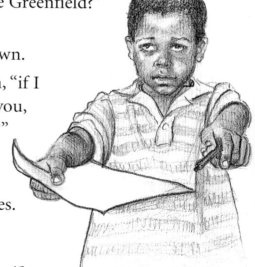

"Okay," I told him, "if I write Greenfield for you, will you stop talking?"

He handed me a sheet of yellow paper with wide, dotted lines.

Greenfield was the name of the town where Tyrone and Lou used to live. I printed the word in big letters. Tyrone nodded and took the paper over to his bed. I started to read.

"Do you have scissors?" Tyrone asked. He held up the paper. "Can you cut this?"

I cut out the word Greenfield and handed it to Tyrone. He looked down and made that funny face, puffing his cheeks full of air.

Then he got ready for bed. He went to sleep the way he did everything else. He rocked in his bed, he talked, and he sang. Noise, noise, noise!

The next day, I left for school before Tyrone was awake. I had a track meet every day that week, and I never got home until after supper. I had to study for two tests, and I had a paper to write. But every night when I tried to do my homework, Tyrone had another question.

"How does a bus work?"

"I'm too busy to tell you about motors, Tyrone."

"No, I mean how do you ride on a bus?"

I glared at him. "You go to the bus stop on Main Street and get on."

Another night he asked, "How much does it cost?"

How much did what cost? What was he talking about?

"The bus," he said, like I should have known all along.

I sighed. "It depends on where you want to go."

"Well, what's the most it could cost?"

"Three dollars." I just made that up so he'd stop asking. ⨾

I saw him look at his money jar on the dresser. Then he made his funny face and looked at the floor.

The next night I was trying to study. Tyrone was bumping around in the closet. I couldn't think straight with all that noise.

"Can't you ever be quiet?" I asked.

He came out of the closet with a suitcase. He held it up and pulled on the zipper to show me that it was stuck. I grabbed the suitcase out of his hand and pushed the zipper back and forth until it worked.

"Do you have any string?" he asked.

I threw an old shoestring on the floor. "Instead of asking me for stuff, maybe you should think about giving things back," I snapped.

Tyrone just looked at me with that funny face of his. He took his suitcase and went back into the closet. I went back to reading my books.

The next night Tyrone was asleep when I got home. I was careful where I stepped in the dark. I didn't want to trip over any of Tyrone's toys. It must have been my lucky night. I didn't trip over a thing.

Chapter 4

A New Ship

Like I said, none of this would have happened if my mom hadn't married Lou. And they didn't even know Tyrone was gone. I was going to have to run around the neighborhood by myself. It was seven o'clock on Saturday morning, and I had to find my new stepbrother, the runaway.

Where could Tyrone have gone? I tried to add up the clues. He had asked me to write down the word Greenfield, and he had asked me about the bus. That was a pretty big hint, but I'd been too busy feeling sorry for myself to notice. I had told a five-year-old kid to take three dollars and get on the bus at Main Street. That bus didn't even go to Greenfield.

I thought about how I'd fixed the zipper on his suitcase. I wanted to smack myself on the head.

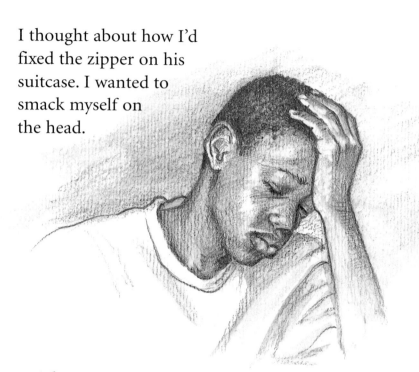

There was no time to go to the park and get my mom and Lou. I had to find Tyrone by myself. It was 7:15. If Tyrone had waited until his dad and my mom were out of sight, he could only have been gone 15 minutes. His suitcase would slow him down.

I turned the two pieces of my old ship over in my hands. I hadn't done a very good job with Tyrone. I could see that. After all, he wasn't the one who decided to move in with us. He probably didn't like sharing a room with me, either.

Maybe there was a chance I could fix things. I grabbed the rest of the ship and went down the stairs three at a time.

As I raced downtown, I worried that Tyrone had gotten lost or hurt. I ran faster than I had in any track meet.

When I was almost to Main Street, I spotted Tyrone. He was pulling his suitcase down the sidewalk. He was a block away from the bus stop. He had tied his little sign for Greenfield around his neck with my old shoestring. He looked really small and kind of sad.

When he saw me coming, he tried to hurry ahead. I heard a bus coming around the corner. I had to think quickly.

"Hey, Tyrone," I called out, "have you seen this one?"

He turned around.

I held out my old ship, then pretended to trip over my own feet. I landed on my hands and knees on the sidewalk in front of him. I did a good job of scattering ship pieces everywhere.

Tyrone put down his suitcase. I could see that he wanted to help. I hoped so.

"It's all broken," he said.

"I really mess things up sometimes," I told him.

The bus stopped at the curb. I moved between Tyrone and the bus door. "Think you can help me fix it?" I asked.

The driver wanted to know if anyone was getting on.

"I'd really like your help," I said to Tyrone.

He looked over my shoulder at the driver. He looked at the ship pieces all over the ground.

"Think we can fix it like it was before?" he asked.

"No," I told him. "Let's make something new." I started picking up the pieces. "Okay?"

Tyrone thought for a minute. He waved goodbye to the bus driver and kneeled on the sidewalk. He reached for a piece of the broken ship. "Okay," he said. "I'll help if you need me."

Me too, I thought. I sat down on the curb next to my stepbrother. Me too.